The Last Mapou

Written by:
EDWIDGE DANTICAT

Illustrated by:
EDOUARD DUVAL-CARRIÉ

ONE MOORE BOOK

Illustrated by Edouard Duval-Carrié
Designed by Steven Melamed

The panels used in this book were enhanced by Augustus Moore Jr.

One Moore Book publishes culturally sensitive and educational stories for children of countries with low literacy rates and underrepresented cultures. We provide literature for children whose narratives are largely missing from the children's book publishing industry. The books also serve as a key to unknown people and places for all children who do not have access to cultures outside of their own.

The One Moore Book Store is a distributor of multicultural children's literature from popular and celebrated authors, as well as new and unknown authors whose narratives serve the needs of readers all around the world.

For more information, please visit www.onemoorebook.com

The Last Mapou

"Our mapou is dying," my grandmother said one morning while we walked through her vast and beautiful garden, far up in the hills above Port-au-Prince.

We walked under yellow oleanders as bright as the sun and spider lilies that really looked like spiders.

We walked; sometimes fast and sometimes slow, past the almond, mango and avocado trees, even though Grann looked a little bit tired.

We then stopped so that

After Grann had rested for a while, she picked a bright red, bell-shaped hibiscus and placed it behind my ear, then we walked again until we reached the back of the garden where the mapou tree stood.

Grann could catch her breath.

My grandmother's mapou tree was the tallest tree I had ever seen. It was two-hundred years old and over a hundred and FIFTY FEET TALL. It was so tall that the top of it seemed to be lost in the clouds. It was so high that it would take a whole day to climb it, though Grann would never let me because sometimes bats made their nest in the mapou's tall branches.

The mapou was SO WIDE that I could not hug it and touch hands on the other side. The leaves were shaped like Grann's and my hands except the leaves were as broad as dishes. The roots were stretched out all over the ground, like snakes slithering away from their nests.

At first, I could not tell what was wrong with the mapou until Grann showed me how many of the leaves had turned brown. The mapou's bark was now so dry it looked like sandpaper, and its roots had also loosened from the ground.

"Each time it rains," Grann said, still a bit out breath, "more of the mapou's legs get pulled apart from their rightful place." That was her way of saying that more and more of the mapou's roots had lost their grip on the earth and soon the mapou would fall on my grandmother's house, unless it was cut down.

"I've done everything I could to save it, "Grann said sadly, "but nothing's worked. The other trees and flowers are thriving, but no amount of care has been able to help the mapou."

I remember how green...

...and strong...

...and beautiful

the mapou had been when
I was much smaller.

Every Saturday morning, Manman and Papa drove me from the city to the hills above Port-au-Prince. There I would spend time with Grann while my parents ran their weekend errands. To me, those Saturday mornings and my grandmother's mapou tree were the most beautiful things in the world. They always made me happy.

Even though she was trying to hide it from me, she didn't seem as well as she'd been on other Saturday mornings when we would do all kinds of fun things together. We would carve small statues of ourselves out of the mapou's branches and embroider dollies and place mats, while swaying back and forth in the rocking chairs on her balcony.

And she would let me
eat whatever cookies and
cake she had around while
she talked with a friend or
two on the phone.

That Saturday morning though, as we walked, each step seemed to tire my grandmother and she kept grimacing as she looked up at the mapou, as though she were in pain.

When she noticed how sad it made

would have to be put down, my grandmother walked

mapou tree and told me

"I know something that will make you feel better, "she said, after catching her breath. "I will tell you the story of the mapou."

"I didn't realize the mapou had a story," I said.

"Everything has a story," Grann said, chuckling. "And this mapou's story goes like this."

me to see her so tired and to hear that the mapou

me over to one of the many benches under the

to sit down next to her.

"Haiti was once a forest on top of a hill, like the hill where this house stands," my grandmother said. "Haiti was once a forest filled with mapou trees. And many people were living inside the trees."

One day a man and a woman, two of our ancestors, got tired of living inside their trees and walked out into the forest. As other people heard their footsteps and laughter in the forest, they too came out of their mapou trees, forming a small village on the hill.

The people in the village used the mapou's light softwood to build houses. They used the fragile white silk fiber around the mapou seeds to make mattresses, which is why some also call the mapou tree a silk cotton tree. They used the mapou's hollowed trunks to make canoes and rafts to fish when they left the hill and moved closer to the sea.

They crushed the mapou seeds and used them to make oil, soap and fertilizer for crops. When anyone got sick, the mapou's sap was used as medicine. The mapou's large white and pink flowers, which bloom only at night, were used to decorate their homes. In the daytime, the flowers drew bees toward them and honey was harvested from the mapou's very wide branches.

When my great-great grandparents were born, their umbilical cords were buried under a mapou tree. When they and their children got married, the marriage ceremony was held under a mapou tree so that each couple could receive the silent blessings of their ancestors.

As time went on, more and more mapous were cut down to build houses and fishing rafts and to make mattresses not only for the growing village, but also the surrounding cities. Now all of the mapou trees on the hill had been cut down, except Grann's.

But that last mapou tree was now sick. We either had to cut it down or let it fall on its own, which could destroy Grann's beautiful house and possibly harm her too.

When Grann was done telling the story, she reached under the bench and pulled out a small cushion she had made when she'd found out that the mapou tree could not be saved. On the cushion, Grann had embroidered tiny pictures that told the story of the mapou tree the way she had just told it to me.

The cushion was stuffed with the silken fibers from the mapou seeds, which made it light and soft when I held it in my hands.

Grann also gave me a small wooden statue of a little girl. The little girl looked exactly like me. The statue had been carved by my grandmother from the honey-colored wood of the mapou tree.

"I want you to have these things," Grann said. "So you will always remember the mapou's story, so that you can also tell it to others."

Holding my grandmother's cushion and statue, my sadness about the mapou and my grandmother's tiredness were lifted.

Later that morning, while sitting on my grandmother's balcony, the one facing neither the garden nor the mapou, but the city, we heard the workmen's very loud saws pruning and scaling off the mapou's branches before they started cutting it down. Neither my grandmother nor I wanted to see the mapou cut down. We both wanted to remember it standing strong and tall, just like in my grandmother's story.

The mapou has been gone for some time now and so sadly has my grandmother. She was as sick as the mapou that Saturday morning, though she did not want to tell me.

Still, sometimes, as I walk through my grandmother's garden, I think I can still hear her voice. It is as if my grandmother's voice is always floating somewhere in the breeze and waiting to land in my ear.

I hear my grandmother's soft chuckle. Then I hear a voice echo through the rustling leaves of the remaining trees, while telling the mapou's story.

This time though I am part of the mapou's story because I am the one telling it.

The End

AUTHOR'S NOTE:

In Haiti the mapou or silk cotton tree is a very important and symbolic national tree. So much so that when someone of great importance and integrity has died, it is often said that "a mapou has fallen". The mapou trees are perhaps the most dramatic victims of deforestation in Haiti. In the 1940's they were cut down by the Catholic Church to discourage the practice of the Vodou religion, of which mapou trees are an integral part. Today, their continued destruction for religious reasons as well as for use in construction and charcoal production, is contributing to the ongoing devastation of Haiti's ancestral, spiritual, and environmental preservation.

THE LIBERIA SERIES

J is for Jollof Rice
Story by Wayétu Moore
Illustrated by Kula Moore

1 Peking
Story by Wayétu Moore
Illustrated by Augustus Moore Jr.

My Little Musu
Story by Wiande Moore-Everett and Wayétu Moore
Illustrated by Kula Moore

Kukujumuku
Story by Wayétu Moore
Illustrated by Augustus Moore Jr.

A Gift for Yole
Story by Wayétu Moore
Illustrated by Augustus Moore Jr.

I Love Liberia
Written by Wayétu Moore
Illustrated by Kula Moore

Jamonghoie
Story by Jassie Senwah-Freeman
Written by Wiande Moore-Everett & Wayétu Moore
Illustrated by Augustus Moore Jr.

THE LIBERIA SIGNATURE SERIES

Gbagba
Written by Robtel Pailey
Illustrated by Chase Walker

In Monrovia, When the River Visits the Sea
Written by Patricia Jabbeh Wesley
Illustrated by Kula Moore

What Happened to Red Rooster When a Visitor Came
Written by Stephanie Horton
Illustrated by Chase Walker

THE HAITI SERIES

The Last Mapou (Also in Kreyol)
Written by Edwidge Danticat
Illustrated by Eduoard Duval-Carrie

Elsie
Written by Cybille St. Aude
Illustrated by Marie Cecile Charlier

A is for Ayiti (Also in Kreyol)
Written by Ibi Zoboi
Illustrated by Joseph Zoboi

Fabiola Konn Konte {Fabiola Can Count}
Written by Katia D.Ulysse
Illustrated by Kula Moore

Where is Lola?
Written by Maureen Boyer
Illustrated by Kula Moore

I am riding
Written by M J Fievre
Illustrated by Jean P. Icart Pierre

CPSIA information can be obtained
at www.ICGtesting.com
Printed in the USA
LVHW07n2311100718
583347LV00006B/25/P